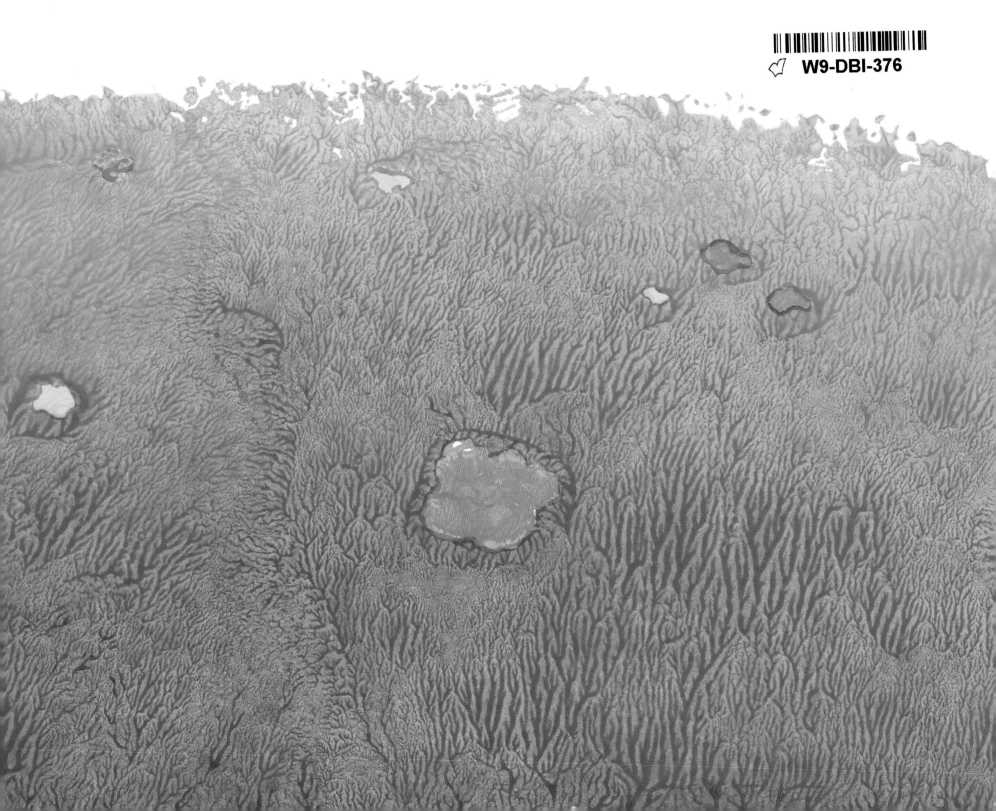

Marcus Pfister was born in Bern, Switzerland. After studying at the Art School of Bern, he apprenticed as a graphic designer and worked in an advertising agency before becoming self-employed in 1984. His debut picture book, *The Sleepy Owl*, was published by NorthSouth in 1986, but his big breakthrough came six years later with *The Rainbow Fish*. Today, Marcus has illustrated over fifty books, which have been translated into more than fifty languages and received countless international awards. He lives with his wife, Debora, and his children in Bern.

First published in the United States, Great Britain, Canada, Australia, and New Zealand
in 2020 by NorthSouth Books Inc., an imprint of NordSüd Verlag AG, CH-8050 Zürich, Switzerland.

Distributed in the United States by NorthSouth Books Inc., New York 10016.
Library of Congress Cataloging-in-Publication Data is available.
Printed at Livonia Print, Riga, Latvia, 2019.
ISBN: 978-0-7358-4417-9
1 3 5 7 9 • 10 8 6 4 2

www.northsouth.com
www.rainbowfish.us
Meet Marcus Pfister at www.marcuspfister.ch

FSC
www.fsc.org
MIX
Paper from
responsible sources
FSC® C002795

MARCUS PFISTER

LEO'S MONSTER

North
South

It was Leo's first trip to the home of his friend Zoe.
He left the city to visit her in her country mouse home.

"I need to check on the cake. You can look around outside if you like,"
suggested Zoe. "But call me if one of the cats comes too close to you."

"I will," said Leo cheerfully, and bounded out into the open air.

When Zoe had taken the cake out of the oven, she went outside to look for Leo.
He came rushing toward her, trembling all over.

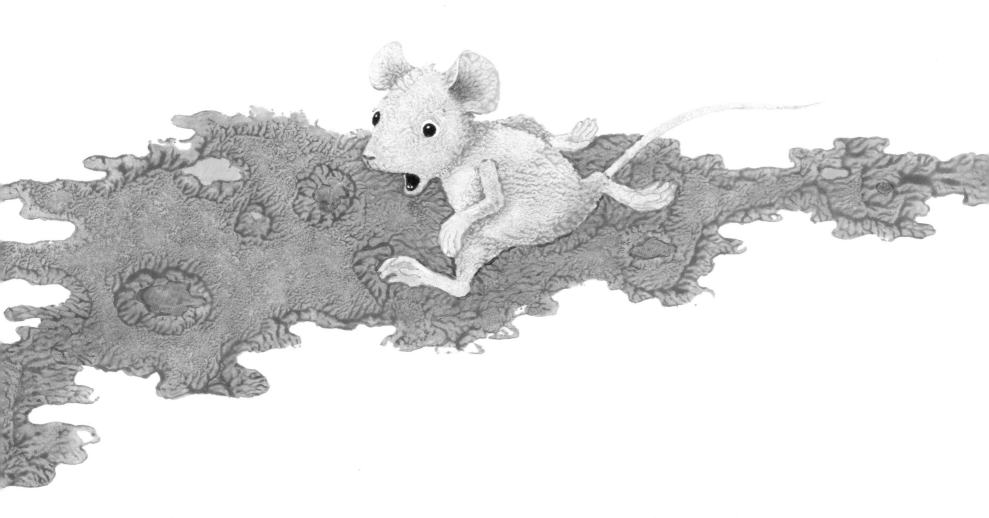

"I-I just saw a m-m-monster!" he stammered, scarcely able to breathe.

"You mean you saw a cat," said Zoe calmly.

"NO, I kn-kn-know what c-c-cats look like!" cried Leo. "It-it was a m-m-monster!"

"WHAT? You really saw a monster?" asked Zoe, eyes wide. "Where? What did it look like? I want to see it too!"

"Are you c-c-crazy?" answered Leo. "It was o-o-over there, in that endless g-g-green. And it had an enorm-enorm-enormous tail, which it used to whip the air. Here, there, and everywhere."

"Okay, okay," said Zoe, trying to calm him down.

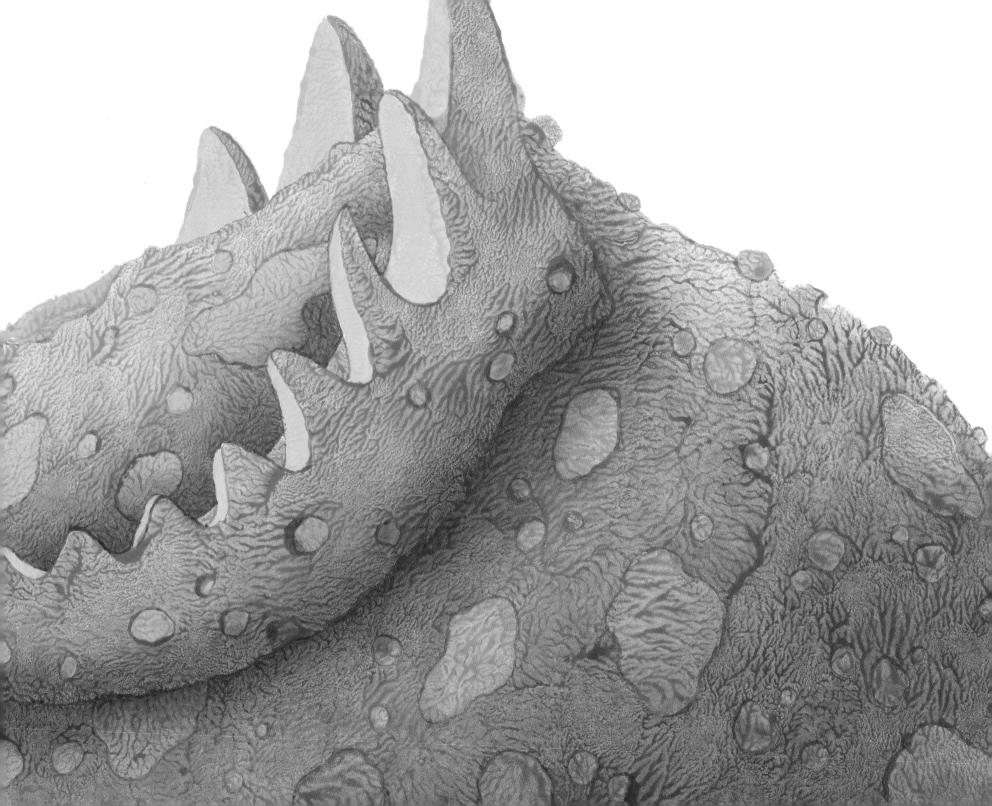

"And he had hard lumpy feet. The monster almost trampled me!
I only just managed to jump out of the way!"

"Really?" asked Zoe in amazement.

"Did it also spit fire?" asked Zoe.

"Don't be silly—it wasn't a dragon; it was a monster!" answered Leo.

"If it had spit fire, I'd hardly be standing here now, would I?"

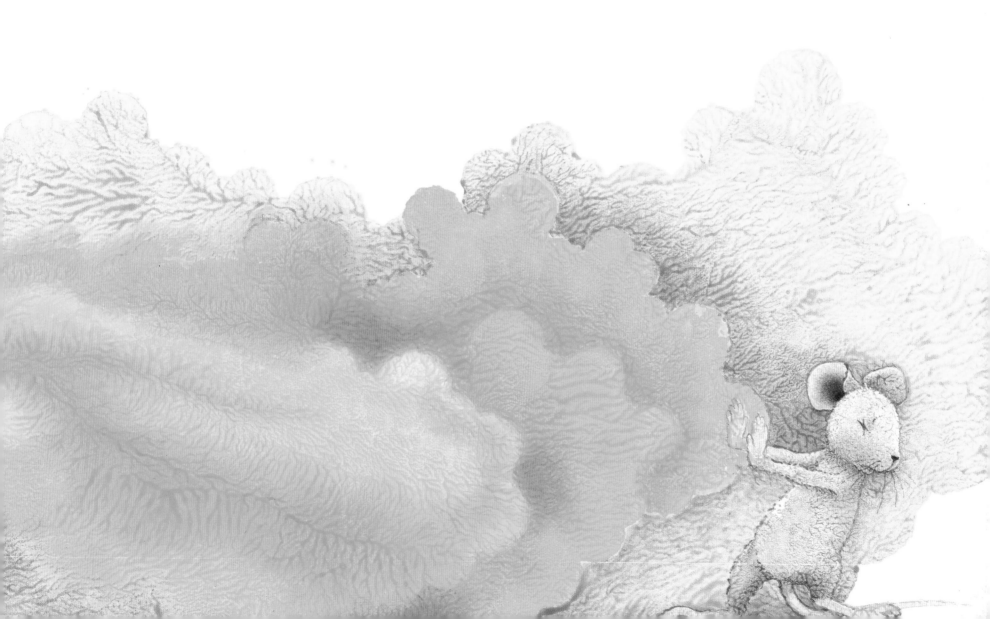

"But it had a tongue— Well, you've never seen anything like it in all your life! Just with its tongue alone it ripped out half the earth. I think the monster could even tear out trees with that tongue!"

"Oh come on, now you really are exaggerating!" objected Zoe.

"No I'm not. It even had two pointed horns and almost gored me!"

"Are you sure it only had two horns?" asked Zoe.

"There might have been more! Oh my!"

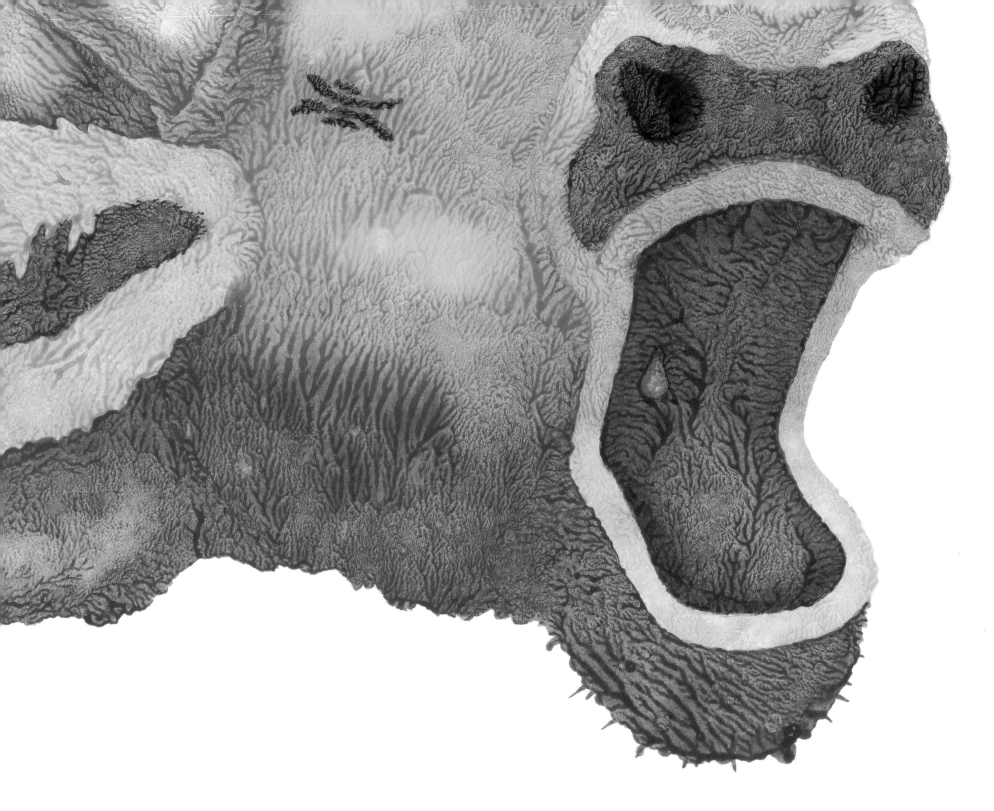

"And it made such a noise!
I had to put my paws over my ears!
It roared so loud that the earth quaked.
I thought my last hour had come...," said Leo,
his voice trembling.

"What did the monster's body look like?"
Zoe wanted to know.
"It was sort of half black and the other half was—"
"Blue?" asked Zoe.

"No, the other half was—"

"Purple?" Zoe interrupted him again.

"No, let me finish, will you?" cried Leo.

"The other half was white. And it stank. Oh, it really stank! It did a liquid poo, as big as a lake!"

"This is a monster I really want to see!" said Zoe with a smile. "Show me the way."

So Leo crept ahead, and Zoe followed close behind.

"By the way," said Zoe helpfully, "that endless green is what we call a field."

"Th-th-there it is … right in fr-fr-front of us," whispered the terrified Leo.

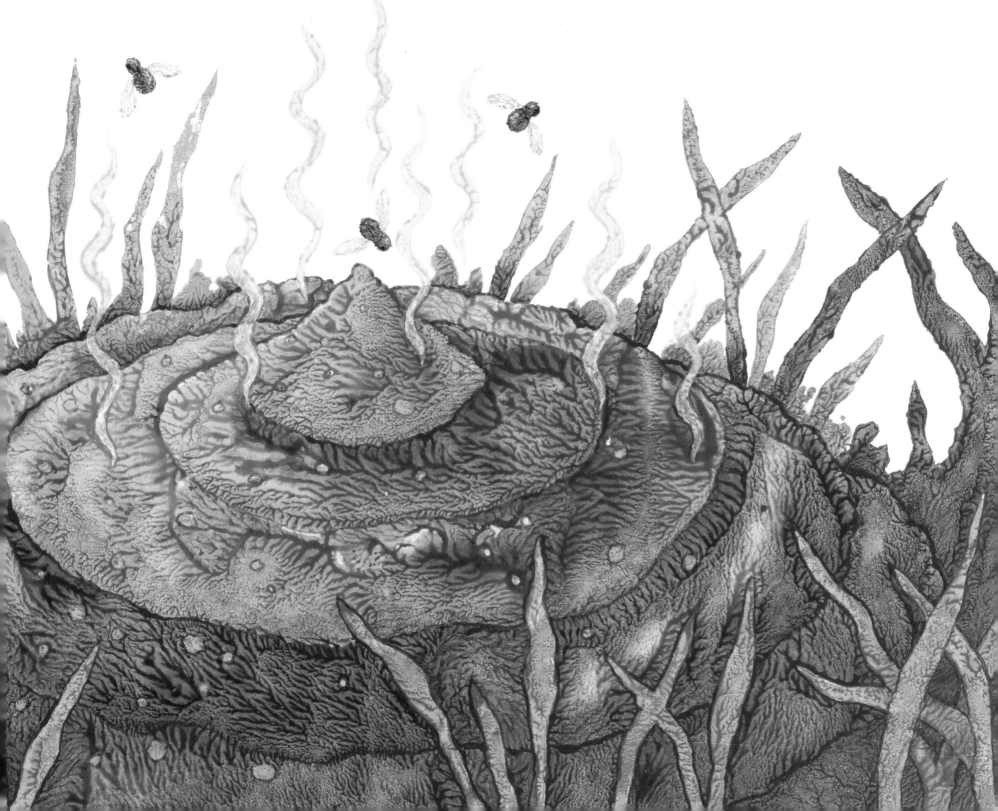

"Hello, Bertha, how are you?"
Zoe asked the farmer's cow.

"Moo!" replied the cow in such a loud voice that the ground shook.

"There's a good monster," said Zoe, patting Bertha's muzzle.

Leo hesitated for a moment, but when Zoe started laughing, he couldn't help laughing too.

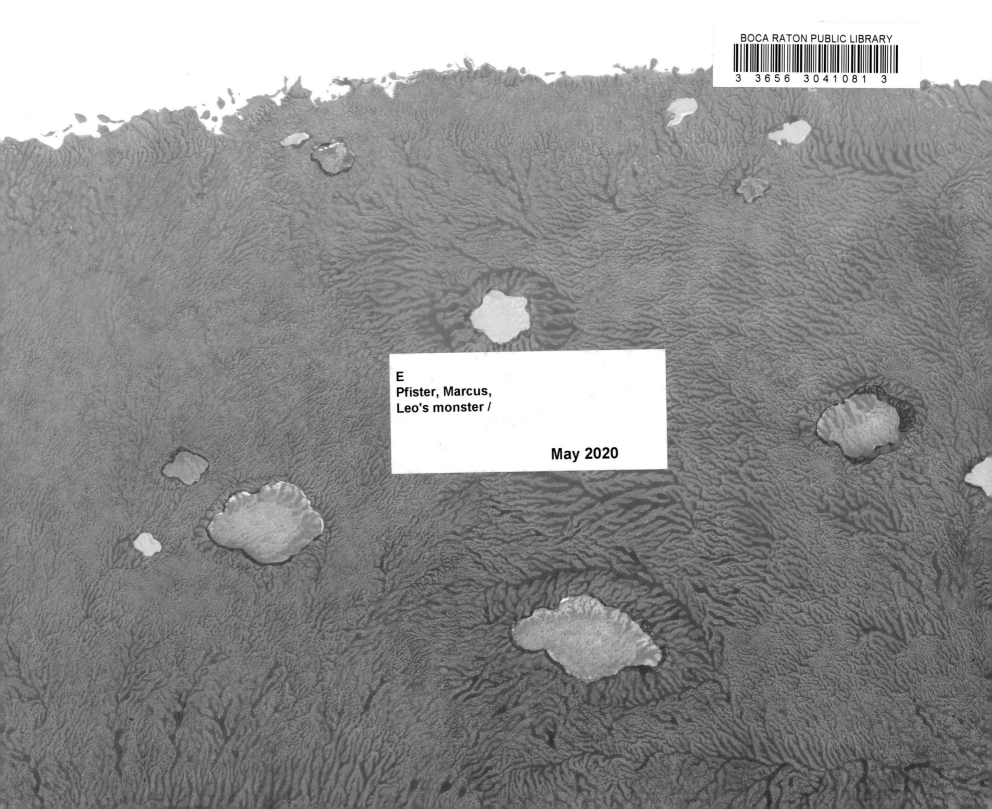